Kedo Publishing, Inc.
11 West Prospect Avenue
Mount Vernon, NY 10550
www.kedopublishing.com

Ordering information:
Quantity sales. Special discounts are available on bulk quantity purchases by corporations, associations and others. For details, contact the publisher at the address above.

Printed in the United States of America

Publisher's Cataloging-in-Publication data
Names: Blair, Kiara A., author. | Richardson, Jenise C., author. | Toons, Oscar, illustrator.
Title: Adventures in Goobieland : Sickybug / by Kiara A. Blair and Jenise Richardson; illustrated by Oscar Toons.
Series: Adventures in Goobieland
Description: Mount Vernon, NY: Kedo Publishing, Inc., 2021. | Summary: Three friends visit a new playpark. It's everything they dreamed of, but they return to Goobieland with something they didn't want at all, a nasty cough! What must they do to make sure other people don't catch it?
Identifiers: LCCN: 2021914034 | ISBN: 978-1-7374376-1-1
Subjects: LCSH Virus diseases--Juvenile fiction. | Epidemics--Juvenile fiction. | Sick--Juvenile fiction. | Influenza--Juvenile fiction. | Social distancing (Public health)--Juvenile fiction. | BISAC JUVENILE FICTION / Health & Daily Living / Diseases, Illnesses & Injuries | JUVENILE FICTION / Animals / General.
Classification: LCC PZ7.1.B5785 Adv 2021 | DDC [E]--dc23

First Edition

Adventures in GOOBIELAND
SICKYBUG

This book belongs to

Over the mountains and far, far away, the people of Goobieland live, work, and play.

One day in Goobieland,
Kiara, Naveah, and Zion the cat
were getting very excited!

They were going on a trip to Tibbletown. There was a new tumblepark in Tibbletown. They couldn't wait to visit.

Kiara had to line up for a long time
to play on the Whizzy-Slide.
But it was worth it.
It was so fast and really fun!

Naveah had to share the Jiggle-Gym with lots of other children. But it was worth it. It was so cool and really fun!

Zion had to take turns with other children to use the Super-Swings. But it was worth it. The swings went up so high, and they were really fun!

But on the way home, Kiara began to cough.
That made Naveah begin to cough.
And that made Zion begin to cough.

By the time they got home, they were all coughing a lot. They all snuggled up under a blanket with a cup of hot Choco-Milk and watched the news.

"NEWS FLASH!" said the reporter. "Everybody in Tibbletown is coughing. They have all caught the Sickybug!"

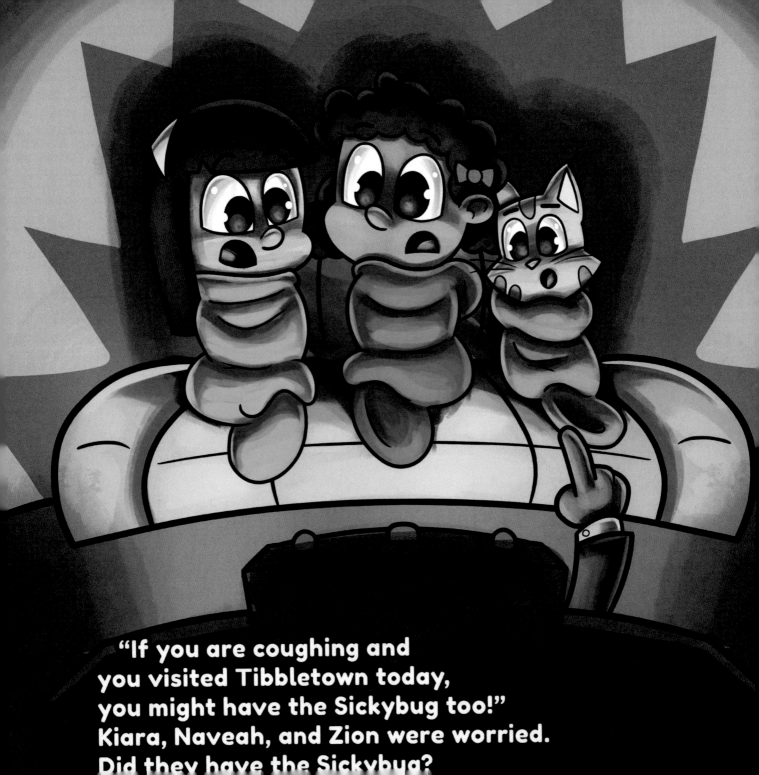

"If you are coughing and
you visited Tibbletown today,
you might have the Sickybug too!"
Kiara, Naveah, and Zion were worried.
Did they have the Sickybug?

Sickybug Update

Samantha: Boss of Goobieland

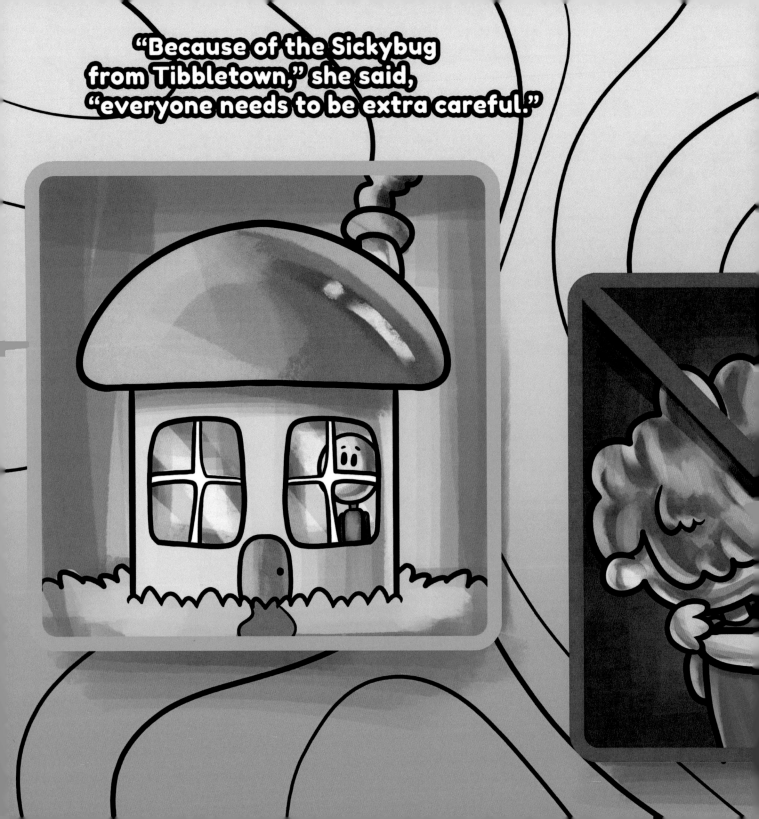

"Because of the Sickybug
from Tibbletown," she said,
"everyone needs to be extra careful."

"If you have a cough, you must stay inside.
If you visit a store, you must wear a mask.
And last of all, no hugging
until the Sickybug is gone."

So Kiara, Naveah, and Zion stayed inside for ten whole days and ten whole nights. It was a bit boring. But it was important not to spread the Sickybug.

Ten days later, when they were feeling much better, Naveah went to the store to buy a Bready-Loaf. She made sure to wear a mask.

Everybody in Goobieland was wearing a mask and staying away from one another. It was a bit strange. But it was important not to spread the Sickybug.

One day, a few months later, Kiara, Naveah, and Zion were watching the news again. "ANNOUNCEMENT!" shouted the voice on the TV.

Made in the USA
Middletown, DE
12 October 2021